TAILS FROM THE CAT SHOP

THE KITTEN'S STORY

JESSIKA JENVIEVE

ABOUT THE AUTHOR

Jan Sayer has worked with some incredibly exciting people who are far too celebrated to be named in her humble biography. She studied English and Drama at the legendary Bretton Hall, an experience which changed her life forever. After two years managing a bookshop, she changed direction, learned a lot of new skills and embarked on tours across Europe as both a company stage manager and a lighting designer.

For a decade, she worked as a stage manager at the Sydney Opera House, served as a producer for the Sydney 2000 Olympic Games, and most recently held the position of executive assistant at the University of Sydney.

She has written two crime thrillers, **Exposure**, set in Nova Scotia, and **We can't all die like Buddy Holly**, a UK regional crime novel.

Today she lives on the island of Texel in the Netherlands. She loves cats, sports cars and the ocean, and hopes to earn enough to feed her designer clothes habit.

She writes the **CyberCat Series** under the pen name of Jessika Jenvieve.

Sign up for the latest news at https://www.jansayer.com/

To Philip, my Dude

'It feels like there is a future'

ABOUT US

Storm and Dude were a **Second Life** partnership. These two quirky individuals spent their Second Lives and a good proportion of their Real Lives together, despite the fiercely opposing time zones. They are not young, but they are certainly not yet old and both have playful natures and a love of cats. **Not Another Kitten** was their first virtual world business.

Storm and Dude spend much of their Second Life at the Junkyard Blues Club, a music, dancing and community venue with a lot of humour, chat and often, flirting and romance. The dance floor is the place where they met, and got to know each other. There are occasionally terrible fights when Dude rants and Storm storms off, but somehow love always won the day.

SECOND LIFE

Second Life is an online virtual world developed by Linden Lab in 2003. Free online viewers enable Second Life users to interact with each other in a world-wide metaverse using avatars. They can explore the world, meet others, socialise, take part in activities, create amazing things, and trade virtual property and services with one another. Built into the software is a three-dimensional modelling tool based on simple geometric shapes (prims) that allow residents to build virtual objects, such as houses and gardens. There is also a scripting language, which can add interactivity to objects, such as breedable animals.

Avatars can communicate via local chat and instant messaging (known as IM). Many residents also meet regularly on Skype. There is streamed music, and many artists perform live in the virtual world venues. Painters and sculptors exhibit and SL poets weave their verses. There are filmmakers who record and broadcast. All creative life is there.

Rezz (in Second Life) means to create or to make an object

appear. If something were to appear out of nowhere, you would say it 'rezzed'.
Urban Dictionary

KittyCatS!

These are highly interactive cats in Second Life that can be petted and cuddled. They will follow you and play with you. There are lots of breeds and sizes, including teacup, toy, petite, normal and MegaPuss. There are also special collection cats that will breed one unique baby. It is compelling, addictive and fascinating.

A BUNDLE OF PIXELS

PHILIP FINLAY BRYAN

Getting a virtual pet in Second Life is quite a remarkable experience. You go to the shop and choose your pet, in this case a cat. You can see the genealogy of your cat. The 'birth' is an experience in itself. You buy a box with your kitty in it and rezz it. You have to wait 15 minutes and you are presented with a dialogue such as 'Your kitty's eyes are just opening and she is fumbling around'. This goes on for 15 minutes detailing what would be the birth of a real kitten. You, well we did, you sit and wait and watch as the box starts to move. Then the kitten is born. A kind of reverse imprinting occurs.

A rapid learning process by which a newborn or very young animal establishes a behavior pattern of recognition and attraction to another animal of its own kind or to a substitute or an object identified as the parent.

The American Heritage Dictionary of the English Language,
4th edition.

The kitten is tiny and has a name. You can see a menu detailing love, happiness, food status and age. You set its area of travel. The kitten can sit on your shoulder during the first week. This is a bundle of pixels. Yet psychological mechanisms are at work here. Throughout Second Life, a process goes on whereby identity is given to an onscreen representation of you. It is a primitive expert system that responds to your input.

This kind of behavior is not uncommon in children. Their toys take on a life of their own with likes and dislikes, a pure projection of the child's imagination. How much more real is having a 'toy' that has a degree of autonomy, but is still dependent on you for love and food in order to grow and live? Bonding occurs. But the bonding is with the avatar so we are even further removed from the actuality. Isn't this wonderful. First, we have identified with the avatar, which becomes an extension of ourselves, and then we anthropomorphize even further to give life to a bundle of pixels.

Philip Finlay Bryan

ONE

ONE
DUDE AND STORM GET A KITTEN
AND THERE ARE GIFTS

THEY FIRST SAW the kittens wandering around the dance floor of Toby's Juke Joint. They didn't squash if you trod on them.

Aw Cute Cute So Cute

Their downfall followed quickly.

Storm was alone and Dudeless that day, when she found the Kitten Barn and there was row upon row of cute kitten pictures and nice little boxes. Throwing caution to the wind, and she came home with a small brown box. Actually, she liked the box, but her addiction to boxes could be another story.

The box sat temptingly on the floor until Dude arrived and wandered round it for a while. They were both nervous. This was to be their first-born kitten, since committing to their partnership following a romantic evening spent by a pool. Let's call that another story too.

They had no clue what they were doing. Storm was very inexperienced when it comes to things giving birth. She saw a goat give birth once, but was away being sick at a critical juncture. Dude is a bit more experienced but easily distracted, as he was often away registering a domain:

```
http://mybabiesfirstdomain.com
```

So here we go:

Select Click Unpack

15 minutes? *Your kitten will arrive in 15 minutes.* They were unprepared for this and watched as the box wobbled and shook and talked back. As with all virtual things, a text hops over the object, telling you what is going on. The tension was unbearable. Later births, filmed by Dude, (don't you hate this? - poor kid forced to watch its birth every time there are visitors) were equally enthralling but far less tense.

So, they waited. *Your kitten has opened its eyes - 5 minutes.* They held hands as far as the virtual world technology allowed. And then the box disappeared, and a tiny speck replaced it.

Welcome Ormond!

Setting up the first kitten was complicated as he dived under the sofa, but they got the hang of it pretty quick. Well, they thought they had. Once settled on Storm's shoulder, he was photographed and praised. She was a nervous kitten's Mum at last. His name was computer generated and in many ways that is the fun, the name is selected by the great big database of fate. Storm's fascination with Ormond continues to this day, as some kittens get big personalities and some don't, and Ormond takes after Dude here. He is bold and personality soaked.

The next day, she raced in-world to see her kitten.
ORMOND?
OMG... Where is he?
The fabulous split-level Japanese-designed Balinese-style pavilion home on the cliffs overlooking the Blake's Sea *breathe* is a minefield for kittens with a range of over 4 meters. There are just too many levels, and all she could see of Ormond was his little name tag floating tragically above the floor. Those of you who are unfamiliar with virtual worlds will just have to untether your imagination here. This is a computer-simulated environment, and Ormond was stuck in the pixel wilderness. Storm tried de-rendering the floor, the surface, and the ocean all in a total panic. De-rending lets you select specific items and make them invisible and would have masses of real-life applications. You don't like the neighbor's fence. Hey, let's de-render it. Don't like the neighbor, we can de-render him too. There was soon nothing left to de-render and still no kitten. If you wait long enough, they come back. But Storm was a new first-time kitten, Mum. What to do? Dude, where are you?

Their friend Abal was online, and Storm cried for help. She would know what to do. And she did. A few expert clicks later and the baby was restored to Storm's arms. She learned that a cat tree or basket would be a good thing to tie Ormond to a central position. Virtual animals wander, but only as far as you let them. To Storm's very real delight, Abal sent a gift of a basket and a cat tree for them to use. The cat tree was red tartan and is still in use and full of kittens. It was a lovely example of the kindness of Second Life friends.

Ormond was safe, and Storm's blood pressure went back to normal. After that episode, she needed a lie down, followed by some kitten location research. Dude made sure her training in this area got used rather a lot in the coming months.

TWO
ORMOND GETS SICK

NOW, before you pronounce them insane, you need to understand the conditioning that goes on with these kittens. Dude wrote a really smashing blog about what goes on in our heads, as we are conditioned to love and nurture our 'bundle of pixels'. He has 1001 websites, so you can read it for yourselves. A few days later, Storm arrived to find Ormond lying on his back with tiny paws outstretched, covered in a blanket complete with a thermometer in his baby jaws. Ormond was sick! Only eleven days old and she had made him sick. What a lousy new first-time kitten Mum she was turning out to be. Check the food.

Yes, we have food.

Dude arrived, alerted by the whimpers and proceeded to be the concerned father by walking around in circles saying idunno, idunno:

`http://idunno.me.`

It was time for the experts at KittyCatS to help.

. . .

Support Ticket: Ormond is sick Age: 11 days Love: 10% Happiness: 8% Energy: 84% Hunger: 100%

He has food, but only 75% has been eaten. I bought pet recovery vitamins, but these failed to work. I confined him to a 4m range and his food bowl is right next to him. We set both cat and all items to my groups. Please help. Storm.

And they did. They were used to first-time kitten parents in total panic. In Second Life, you can set the ownership of objects to a group so group members can share them. Storm had set Ormond to one group and his food to another. That was wrong. They gently explained and calmed her. He was reset and given special vitamins and a miraculous recovery happened.

This was a real lesson for us all in the psychology of pixel possession. Dude knows about these things. He looked calm and chanted some useful mantras, but he had the same sinking feeling as Storm. They had failed their first kitten and he survived.

Phew!

Dude was, by this time, getting a bit fed up with Ormond and Storm, cuddling all the time. As soon as Ormond got over his sickness, Storm began to suffer from the 'only giraffe in the wildlife park' syndrome. She got this first many years ago after a trip to a Wildlife Park in Norfolk. There was only one giraffe for no apparent reason. Did they eat too much, or did they fight? Who knows, no one was telling and there, in the corner of a damp English field, was this poor creature from Africa standing mournfully under an inedible tree with no intelligent conversation to be had in his own language this side of Regent's Park Zoo.

Storm was extraordinarily sad and needed the comfort of an ice cream.

It was at that moment that she realized that Noah's Ark had two of everything, not only for procreation, but because we all need a pal who speaks our language. Storm has Dude now, but wonders sometimes about his language. He often drops into Japanese and waves his arms, and she can't understand a word. C'est la vie.

So poor Ormond was lonely. A trip to the Kitten Barn and another tension-filled 15 minutes produced the beautiful Bronya with her lovely dark fur and secret Siamese trait. It was love at first sight for the two cats. Not much else on offer, perhaps. Dude was secretly plotting his own kitten and after a few days of 'Do you think I should get a kitten?' as he circled his island, they went to the Kitten Barn together and he spent ages choosing his first pet. Storm stood around, resisting the urge to get another.

So back to Dude's Island for the opening of the box, which he filmed, of course. When Jiselle appeared, he was really delighted and took her everywhere. He crashed a few times, and she had to be retrieved by the nice people at KittyCatS, but he seemed thrilled with her. The love of his life was yet to be born. But we are getting to that soon.

It was a Sunday, and Storm was alone in her house holding Bronya, when looked down and a small box dropped onto the floor. Bronya announced (in chat) that she had a kitten. Storm felt like the cat's grandmother! Frantic emails went out to wake Dude to come and celebrate the birth. She checked on the pedigree, and it was a boy!

Storm thought perhaps Dude might want the new baby as Jiselle was now wandering around his Island looking a bit lonely and forlorn.

THREE

RANDOLPH IS BORN AND DUDE MEETS THE BUDDHA OF INFINITE LIGHT

THEY HAD A WEEKEND OF INDECISION. Dude circled his Island wistfully, looking at his peacocks, motorbike, horse, dog, seagulls, and swans and lovingly patting his collection of Buddhist paraphernalia. Jiselle waited patiently, soon got too big to be carried on his shoulder and was clearly in need of a bonk. Now Storm was not particularly in tune with the sexual needs of those around her, but she knows when a girl wants a bonk! Dude, like most males, is blissfully unaware of this, so even if Jiselle and Storm turned up wearing only high heels and a small hat, he would think their clothes were in the wash. Men can be very strange sometimes. In Storm's opinion, Mars may be too close, or in Dude's case, it's another galaxy entirely.

Finally, he said, yes, he wanted the kitten, and Storm handed over the little brown box. There was now had a regular birthing ritual to follow. They both sat on the sand and metaphorically held hands while Jiselle sat beside them reading her new copy of *The Orgasm Primer*.

There was a genuine air of excitement this time, as they waited to see Bronya and Ormond's first kitten. They had not yet got the hang of reading the pedigree and knowing what was in store. It was still a surprise then, and now, though no longer a surprise, it remains a delight. Bronya, she of the beautiful fur, is a champagne Burmese with azure blue eyes and Ormond is a Blue Tabby with passion red eyes. So, they were not sure what to expect and then the box *poofed* and there was Randolph, a cute carbon copy of Bronya, except he was a petite! Now size in breedables really does not matter, it pops up or down in random sequence. You can breed a teacup size kitten and get a MegaPuss. The gods deal with this.

Randolph was kitten-sweet and once on Dude's shoulder they were inseparable for a week. Then, after a week or two, Jiselle and Randolph both faded from view. Storm guessed they were behind the tent with *The Primer*. The focus shifted to the arrival of the next kitten, Leona Supermodel, a cute carbon copy of her father, Ormond, but with her mother's azure blue eyes.

The breeding program was beginning to seem a tad conventional. Rogue genes were definitely needed. So, while Dude was off registering his 1002nd website, it left Storm at a loose end to explore the kitten markets. She tended to start with the bargain bin, to buy that kitten no one else wants. She was a bit of a soft touch for strays. And then a cute, unwanted red and white Tabby caught her eye. He had pleasant meadow green eyes, was plump, and oh so cute and cuddly. Two clicks later and Storm squirreled him to her cliff-top home and like a naughty girl doing something shocking that she learned in *The Orgasm Primer*; She opened the box....all by herself.

Storm felt a bit guilty that Dude missed out on the hand-holding this time, but the results were so delightful. The kitten was called Amita. This is really a girl's name, which means infinite in Sanskrit and is a word stem of Amitabha, *The Buddha of Infinite Light*.

Dude would really like this little guy, and he was as cuddly and gorgeous as his picture. And the cream on the top? He had wonderful colored parents, one lime green and one grape. The new boy really was special.

FOUR

THE DIVINE PENNY ARRIVES

THEIR SECOND LIFE wandered on in the usual way. Dude's domain empire grew, and they both got more and more skilled with the kittens. The lovely people at KittyCatS were getting a rest from them for a while. It finally occurred to them to look behind the tent to see what Randolph and Jiselle had gotten up to. Both kittens were enjoying a cigarette and a nice brown box was waiting for them. Clearly, these two had been having a bit of a bonk. Storm checked the contents, and both gasped. It was a Siamese! Looking at the pedigrees, they realized that Bronya, bless her beautiful fur, was the carrier of a Siamese trait. Dude was in an overexcited phase because of domain indulgence and instead of clicking UNPACK, he hit OPEN.

There followed a silence in which Storm had to bite her tongue and then ask gently what he had done. She walked him through the contents of his inventory and there was the much-awaited Siamese in lots of pieces. They were both very silent, as they wanted this kitten very much. Dude was feeling much worse than Storm, so she tried not to criticize him too much.

He submitted a ticket to the lovely people at KittyCatS who had likely encountered this type of disaster before. The next day they returned the box unopened, and they had their new kitten ready to birth. There was an air of anticipation on the island as they took up their usual places on the sand and the other cats gathered around. Storm guided Dude's hand as he clicked UNPACK. Fifteen minutes of box shaking and hand-holding, and there she was at last.

Welcome Penrose! Penrose? Penrose!!!

'What sort of name is Penrose?'

Dude was not impressed that the blue-eyed beauty on his shoulder should be called Penrose. It had some kind of fat cartoon animal implications for him, which meant nothing to Storm, who rather liked the name. But she was his kitten, so he changed the name to Penny.

To say this was love at first sight would be a complete understatement. Penny spent her first week on his shoulder. He took her to work in the club, and danced romantically while her fur went up Storm's nose. He gazed at her adoringly, played with her and petted her. Storm tried a whole range of seductive outfits, but unless she was a choc-point Siamese with bright blue eyes, she might as well have given up. Storm has not worked out her allure for him, but it remains still. He looks for Penny when he arrives, and says casually, 'Oh, hello Storm, where's Penny?' .

But Storm was already cooking up schemes to do some breeding, in the hope she could create the mysterious and much prized lime-green Siamese. Jiselle and Randolph, having discharged their duty, remain secretive and secluded. She wondered what they are doing?

Back at Storm's fabulous split-level Japanese-designed Balinese-style pavilion home on the cliffs overlooking the Blake's Sea *breathe*, everyone was breeding in a very unexciting way. Bronya was happily producing substantial quantities of blue Tabbies, and a Château cat, all with interesting 18-carat gold eyes. They birthed the Château, Bryana with her lovely gold eyes and black and white markings, and Aukena, a blue Tabby also with gold eyes, a trait passed from Bronya's grandmother. Leona Supermodel had produced a whole range of unremarkable blue Tabbies. The boxes were piling up in the corner.

Checking again on Amita's impressive pedigree, Storm asked Dude, if Penny might breed with him, Amita, that is. Had Penny been human, Dude would have waltzed down the aisle with her the minute she had finished her Master's degree. That cat needed a bit of motherhood to knock off the innocent allure.Storm broached the subject gently and got the same response you get from a parent if you invite Justin Bieber to visit a girls' boarding school to stay overnight. He bristled quite a lot. So, Storm got out the visual aids and showed him Amita's very splendid parents, **KittyCatS Second Birthday Special Collection** grape and lime cats. Penny nestled in his arms as she did most days and sneered at Storm with her big blue eyes. She would leave her cat toys on the floor for Storm to trip over real soon.

Finally Dude agreed Amita might sleep over and went home to put on his best blue collar and get him ready for his date. Once installed on the island, the cats were partnered and the wait began. Penny continued to walk round with her nose in the air, the sun sparkling on her pristine, creamy fur. Amita sat looking cute with his lovely bright red fur and posh blue collar. He was handsome and the miserable cow was ignoring him. During the night when Dude was in the club, Penny may have tripped on the now discarded and heavily thumbed copy of *The Orgasm Primer*, landed with her paws akimbo, and Amita, the Buddha's sublime cousin, had pounced. Penny was having a kitten at last.

The unpacking of the kitten had all the ceremonies of a Royal Birth. They knew it was a Château cat and a boy. This would be the second Château cat, and Dude had given him to Storm as a partner for her Château cat, Bryana, with the 18-carat gold eyes. Dude fidgeted and wriggled and he registered a couple of sparkly new domains to ease his tension. They sat composed and watched the box hopping about on the sand. When the little black and white speck appeared Storm locked on to him and put him gently on her shoulder for a closer look and the obligatory baby photos.

Welcome Piddles!

Piddles? Dude huffed. Not Piddles, it is Pidder. His name is Pidder. Oh yes, so it was. But her subconscious mind had named the kitten, Piddles. So Piddles, he became. Dude was glad when she took him home and left him to comfort the Divine Penny.

FIVE

PRESENTS AND CHÂTEAU CATS

WITH PIDDLES' arrival, they now had a second Château cat, those nice black and white domestic cats that roam France dining on gourmet mice. The rest of the tribe was happily breeding Tabbies and Burmese in quantity, but they were still yearning for the elusive lime-green Siamese, and no amount of genetic manipulation seemed to get them any closer. Then they got a couple of special kittens to play with. Eberhardt and Treise are Firestorm Third Birthday cats. Firestorm is the virtual world viewer that everyone loves and it was their third anniversary. Group members could get a special kitten with beautiful flame markings. Once the two Firestorm kitties had grown, they took their place as decorative features as they do not breed. Eberhardt lies on his back in the fountain. It seems appropriate for a kitten covered in flames.

Real Life can get busy. Dude has his domain empire to look after and Storm has Professor Poppett, who, as you will all know, wrote *The Orgasm Primer*. We expect her latest work to be a companion volume called *Men and the Lost*

Sock Location Manual. Storm fears that Prof P is confused about the secret ways of the male sex. Dude could explain it to her, but she frightens him terribly. Storm is already anxious as to her part in the research program, searching for Dude's socks in the dark recesses of their Second Life laundry with the animated washing machine. It can be time-consuming and frequently involve unnecessary vibrations.

Professor Poppett does not know about the cats. She might find it slightly strange, so Storm is forced to hide the breeding charts from her eagle eyes, lest she gives her, 'I got up at 5am then rowed up the harbor and now I am running the universe' look. Storm fears it greatly.

Diversity, another Prof P keyword, was the answer, so Storm sneaked off to the cat market bargain bin and found Raynor, a Balinese Seal Lynx, with a creamy coat, stripy socks, blue eyes and perky ears. He would do nicely, so Raynor joined the flock.

Dude was dissatisfied with the name for reasons best only kept in his dark Buddhist past. Storm was satisfied, particularly with his Bengal and Abyssinian ancestors, so they put Raynor to work to enliven the gene pool. There is something excessively male about Raynor. Storm hesitated to call him a 'Stud', but he seems to have leanings towards that role.

They were going through a bit of breeding spurt. Dude was wandering around, telling Storm she had too many kittens and every time his cats presented another box, he opened it. They both had too many mouths to feed and their inventories were bursting with Burmese and Château cats in vast quantities.

Posh Penny peered down from her pedestal and proved

very difficult. They wanted Siamese cats but seemed to have a shortage and a lack of breeding commitment from the kittens. Randolph and Jiselle were now popping out little Burmese and they would have to wait awhile for another Siamese to spend a week draped over Dude's shoulder while he drooled on its tail.

So what to do about all these beasties? Clearly, they could not open the boxes, and had no space or food for anymore. There is a special place called The Menagerie where happy kittens gambol in green meadows with an inexhaustible supply of rare butterflies to be caught, played with, and eaten. A happy land of caviar, kitten kibble and playful fun. It costs nothing to send your little one 'to live Happily Forever in The Menagerie', once sent never to return! Which, in plain, blunt English, is the delete button. Storm was not quite ready for this step - the old pixel conditioning was very strong. Plus, she suspected Dude would hate her for a week and there would be.... DRAMA!

So, the answer was to sell the surplus. They were rather unimpressed with the available-to-rent market stalls. They lacked the personal designer touch and they wanted a sort of Prada of cat shops..... a proper shop.

Storm and Dude spend a lot of time at the Junkyard Blues Club. Junkyard Blues is an outdoor blues club set in a Gulf Coast environment in the virtual world of Second Life. Dude works as host for different blues DJs and Storm stands around decoratively repelling a continual stream of suitors who send messages of appreciation. It is a genuine community in a virtual world, where people share a lot of their personal life and stories. It is also one of the most beautiful places in Second Life, and has been lovingly built and maintained by the owners, Kiff and Dina. It is a testament to the really good people of Second Life.

Along, the canal next to the club is a small row of shops and Dude found just what they were looking for. **Not Another Kitten** had found a home, and they were ready to set up shop.

SIX

THE CAT SHOP OPENS, AND PROFESSOR POPPETT'S POODLE SEES THE THERAPIST

OPENING A SHOP CAN BE STRESSFUL. Storm and Dude took possession of the new shop, which closely resembled the woodcutter's cottage from a fairy tale. The name, **Not Another Kitten**, was completely logical, as Dude had been saying this to Storm for weeks as his tribe of cats took over and rampaged around his Island. Storm found a cute picture of a cat praying to be relieved from the torments of motherhood and installed lots of nice wooden display stands. It was not so much like Prada, but more Ralph Lauren in his highly praised Martha's Vineyard inspired collections featuring healthy blondes with snow-white teeth reclining in gingham evening gowns. The blondes, not the teeth, that is.

Dude created the signs, and all went smoothly, until they were both were pulled up by the estate manager for exceeding the prim allowance. Prims are the building blocks of a virtual world. A lot of boxes were relocated back to Storm's cliff top abode and stored in the newly created library for well-educated pets. A couple of days of math followed until all were settled and they could place gently

Leona Supermodel in the middle of the floor to roam, preen and display herself.

Then there was a DRAMA!

This occurred in the form of the very bad news that Professor Poppett's poodle had developed 'the indoor barking syndrome'. This led to a few stressful days for Storm as the Professor kept falling asleep in her meetings because of extreme tiredness and had to be revived with a glass of the finest red wine. Storm spent most of the week sourcing the rare and delicious liquid and was soon equally exhausted from shopping and tipsy from testing the quality. Dude retreated into another domain:

`http://omgtheyarepissed.org.`

Storm finally fell asleep at the keyboard and all looked very shaky. Dude, being the expert on therapies, suggested that there were a series of options:

- get rid of the poodle,
- send Storm on holiday to Bali,
- or consult a behavioral therapist.

The first was completely against his principles and would upset Storm, and probably Professor Poppett, a good deal more. The second option delighted Storm, who scampered around, until Dude said he could not spare her at this delicate moment in the business venture, so there was absolutely no question of sending anyone to Bali. Storm sulked and was lovingly rewarded with:

`http://myimaginaryholidayinbali.net.`

The last option was chosen, and an expensive therapist was flown in from Alaska, where he had perfected his craft on packs of huskies, who were never known to bark indoors, having never been there.

Spectacular results were expected.

SEVEN

WE MEET JOYOUS JOY, MILLIONAIRE MIJ AND THE RIGHT ROYAL PRINCESS NAO

HAVE you heard about Joyous Joy yet? Joyous Joy is fun size. She is the kitten's friend. She is a peal of bells at a wedding. She is a light bubble of bounce and beauty. When Storm needs a shoulder to cry on, she is there. Soon Joyous Joy came to inspect the cat shop. She pinched each kitten gently to check their plumpness and pronounced them 'very fine kittens'. Storm smiled at this because they were all the same size and still in the boxes, but approval from Joyous Joy was like having the food inspector approve your cupcakes. It was necessary and essential. It was the 'Joyous Joy Seal of Quality'.

That same day, evil loomed over the Cat Shop in the horrible, monstrous shape of Texan Bugg. He got his name, he said, because he was famous for owning a Volkswagen Beetle. Storm could not understand how anything that large could have fitted into a VW, but that is what he said. Dude and Texan Bugg were mortal enemies, which was daft as Dude was as sweet as they come. Texan Bugg was a DJ, and he was back in the Junkyard, and he loved DRAMA!

And he hated kittens...

The shop shook, and the kittens hid in terror when his ugly shadow loomed in the doorway. Leona Supermodel hissed bravely and her little paws shook with fear at the same time. The sounds of his rasping, gurgling laughter filled the air as he wobbled away towards the swampy part of the bayou. He really **hated** kittens. Storm and Dude decided they would watch carefully over their cats if he came that way again. And they would never, ever allow him to buy a kitten. They both shuddered at the thought of its probable fate.

Twins are very rare in the breedable cat world. They cannot be predicted or planned for. There are no genes or traits to show them. They are a gift from the gods. So, when Penny announced that she and Amita had given birth to twins, there was a moment of suspense as Storm stared incredulously at the screen and instinctively called Dude to check she was awake. Dude arrived and had a 'how did this happen' moment, as if he would have to feed and support twins for 18 years or so. They decided that the twins should be the central display of the shop, and Storm was tasked with pricing them. These were not identical twins, so it seemed logical that they should be twice the price of one kitten of the same brand. But they didn't know for sure.

Kitten enthusiasts are friendly types and there was among the Junkyard Blues Club DJs the greatest kitten enthusiast of all. He was known as Millionaire Mij. His kitten empire was vast, and they were all stored neatly in rows. Storm and Dude kept theirs on the window ledge in an untidy pile. Millionaire Mij had exclusive breeds; Devil-Cats, MegaPuss and Foxies. All were rare and beautiful and completely useless at mousing.

His wealth was thought to be because of his superior

social and business connections. Millionaire Mij was the partner of the Right Royal Princess Nao. Her aristocratic antecedents were a little vague, but Dude said that they frequently conversed in a dialect of Siamese Thai, which he had learned in Thailand, so she must be really posh. Storm has a sneaking suspicion that Dude actually came from Park Lane and not the East End of London. He seemed to have a moveable birthplace, so Storm assumed that the ambulance carrying his mother drove around a bit before settling on the exact place of birth. A bit like the Baby Jesus without the census forms to complete. She, on the other hand, had been born in her grandmother's front bedroom, which explained her cheerful disposition and love of Pre-Raphaelite paintings.

There was still the question of the value of twins to be decided and Storm got the landmark of a cat market, where Millionaire Mij had seen some identical twins. Off she went to search. The market was vast and kittens of all shapes and types and colors and prices were piled high on the stalls. Storm's heels clicked on the cobblestones as she systematically searched for the twins. Finally, two matching Siamese were found with a big TWINS label. They were $2500 Linden dollars. Wow!

Resisting the temptation to buy the twins, Storm found a small pink Château boy was somehow purchased and slipped into her shopping basket. No need to tell Dude about that one.

A minor squabble took place when the price was reported, but as they were not identical, the lovely twins were given their 'We are Special' label and proudly displayed for L$800. The pink Château boy was opened in the traditional way.

· · ·

Welcome Hadar!

EIGHT
STORM YEARNS FOR A DEVIL-CAT
AND DUDE PLANS A CUDDLE

HALLOWEEN ARRIVED EARLY that year as the actual day fell midweek, allowing for an entire week of crazy dressing-up in Second Life. The costumes were unusually gorgeous and there was no need to wear the old, dreary, sexy witch costume. Dude wore a very attractive demi-skeleton outfit, which made everyone feel a little queasy, and Storm had a feathery burlesque costume that was presumed to be made from the birds of the Junkyard bayou, which made Dude sneeze. Dressing-up can be a whole lot of fun.

Later in the week she found a stunning bloodstained bridal gown with strategically placed scissors. This was particularly gorgeous and a selection of anonymous, unsolicited floral tributes arrived. Dude growled because he had not sent the flowers, but pretended he had, and then complained that the scissors kept prodding his heart when they danced. Storm said it would likely have no ill effects on him in his stage of decomposition. She smiled smugly because she had received a lot of roses. The kittens stared suspiciously and hungrily at the display of internal organs and the Junkyard dogs waited for Dude to have an unguarded moment.

This was a week of decisions for **Not Another Kitten**. Two of the best breeders retired. Ormond and Bronya reached the 120-day mark and could breed no more. The trip to The Menagerie was not to be for them and Storm bought two lovely plump cushions and they retired to the fountain courtyard with the Firestorm kitty, Eberhardt. They would eat less now separated from the voracious mouths in the other part of the garden.

Millionaire Mij brought his Devil-Cats to the club. These wonderful colored affairs had super pointy ears and little forked tails. They were expensive, and Storm fell instantly in love with them. He had two; one red and one blue and their kaleidoscopic coats flashed and pulsed to the music. Storm was jealous and suspected some of Princess Nao's vast fortune was involved in the purchase.

It was time to survey the breeding stock and work out a strategy. Storm said that Professor Poppett was very keen on strategies and all things strategic, so they must be a good idea and therefore **Not Another Kitten** should have some too. Dude was unsure of the logic here, but he was never sure of Storm's logic, anyway. Storm seemed to lean towards the Siamese so she decided at a board meeting that they should send the Châteaus to the shop, unless they were pink; the Tabbies to The Menagerie, with some of the Burmese and the breeding pairs, should be Siamese or pink Châteaus.

Dude opened his mouth to give his opinion, at which point Bryana and Hadar gave birth to a delicious pink Château cat, and it was time to celebrate. The Divine Penny would be really annoyed about that.

So having one wonderful pink kitten, Hadar, and

another to birth, the planned colored breeding program was ready to go. Dude said on the weekend after Halloween, they should schedule 'a cuddle'. Storm thought this was an excellent plan as there were an awful lot of kittens and if you don't cuddle them, well, they don't, do they? She started a spreadsheet and entered everyone's name. Including the two doing advertising duties at the shop, there were about twenty all up. Fifteen minutes was the minimum cuddle time required to stimulate the breeding and so that would take about 5 hours to get through all of them. If they cuddled two each, it would take about two and a half hours. That seemed reasonable, so the schedule was issued to Dude, who seemed a bit confused to begin with. Then he laughed and said, 'Not them, you daft tart. I mean you'.

(Tart - I should make it very clear is a term of endearment used by those from London, and merely means sweetheart).

Storm had a brief flutter at this. Being a Second Life Partner can be a strange situation. It often means that you love someone who lives, often in another country and time zone. You are unlikely to meet, but you talk to them every day, and see them daily on Skype. And you love this person, just as if they were in the kitchen putting the kettle on. There are enormous advantages to this partnering system. Storm didn't 'do domestic'; being a bit of a career-driven princess, and Dude was saved from Storm's cooking, which was lethal. Their domestic arrangements on Second Life were separate too, as Dude had his Buddhist enclave on an island and Storm had her cliff-top paradise left to her by a former departed partner by way of compensation for forgetting to mention his wife and several children.

They met every day when Dude woke and said Goodnight when Storm was falling asleep. In so many ways, it was completely perfect. There was the horrible physical longing to be dealt with and garment zips that got stuck when there was no one around to help out. Being grown-ups, they managed, and the thought of Storm without Dude or Dude without Storm was like Pinky without The Brain. So, scheduling cuddle time was a very special treat when they would both lie down and share everything in their hearts with each other. It feels like there is a future.

NINE

STORM AND DUDE HAVE A CUDDLE
AND THE DEVIL-CATS ARRIVE

IT IS NOT SEEMLY, as Jane Austen might say, to go into the exact details of the cuddle, other than to note that they were both soon tired and fell asleep.

'Loving someone is giving them the power to break your heart but trusting them not to.' - Julianne Moore.

Dude dreamed of PowerPoint presentations and Storm had an alarming dream in which the Professor of Chemistry, waving his Bunsen burner and yelling about hydrocarbons, was chasing her around the Quad. She woke the next morning to dark skies and rain in the Emerald City where she lived. Knowing that Dude was nicely tucked up counting algorithms, she went for a trip to buy a devil-cat. These come in male or female and you take your chances with the colors and patterns. She bought a male cat and raced home to put the box on the window ledge. First, there was a wonderful flaming heart-shaped box with a forked tail with heaps of food and gifts inside. She pulled out the kitten box and opened up the image to look.

Her new baby was black, with one purple eye and one green eye, green whiskers and a lot of swirling patterns. WOW! Now she had to wait for Dude to wake up and convince him he wanted a devil-girl and they would have a breeding pair. Then, they could open their boxes together like they were both having a birthday. Storm would prepare a feast, actually, maybe not; even virtual kittens would not eat her cooking. Devil-Cats are fiery and beautiful, but they don't breed with the other cats in case their little paws get burnt. So once birthed, these two would be partners.

To pass the time, she opened the pink female kitten with the 18-carat gold eyes, the latest daughter of Amita, the Buddha of Infinite Light, and Bryana; the union of red Tabby and golden- eyed Château cat. Hadar, the pink Château, would need his partner soon as he was growing fast. The new kitten was oh so pink and small and sweet.

Welcome Coconut!

Finally, Dude appeared, shaking his flow charts and muttering arithmetically. While he walked up and down admiring the devil-kitten, it was clear that this would be easy. He wanted a devil-kitten right now. So, about ten minutes later, a second fiery box was on the window ledge. His devil-girl was gold and orange, with glowing eyes. From here, there was simply no stopping them. They clicked the boxes in unison and a race began to see whose kitten arrived first.

Welcome Eckerd and Duvessa!

TEN

WE MEET PRONVELLE, SNEEZE AND THE MOUNTAIN LION

PRONVELLE IS AN INTERESTING GUY. Here are some known facts about him; he is a champion skier, an ocean-racing yachtsman, a lover of cats and a DJ with his own radio station. He wears headbands. He is also on the death list of a very big and dangerous Mountain Lion which lives close to his home in the mountains of Washington State. You get the irony here. He loves cats and they love him, but one of their relatives wants to kill him. It seems a bit like he has upset the Mafia branch of the feline family.

When Pronvelle comes to the cat shop, all the little boxes vibrate, and the sound of soft purring can be heard. They absolutely love him. They get excited by his mere presence and then the purring starts. Storm was told he has the same effect on women, but had no evidence other than her own involuntary purrs when he is around. He has a legendary cat called Sneeze, which is the reason for his being on the Mountain Lion's hit list. Sneeze is on the lunch menu and Pronvelle will shoot at anything that harms his beloved cat. So, in the snow-drenched region where he lives, Pronvelle checks each morning for the big paw prints in the snow and finds that the beast has circled his house ten or twenty times during the night, searching for a way in, or on the off-chance of someone coming out.

Sneeze, of course, is not daft. He is not planning to be anyone's après-ski Rocky Mountain mule deer buffet. So knowing he was dealing with one very bright cat, the Mountain Lion has settled on the larger, more nutritious meal and Pronvelle takes out the garbage armed with a rifle.

Most nights, Sneeze can be found supine on the keyboard while Pronvelle plays a wonderful selection of blues from his part of the USA. This is really special music as most of it has been recorded live. It is quirky, original and fun. Pronvelle has a voice like a chocolate cake with extra cream. There is no other DJ like him and Texan Bugg often lurks around, hoping to learn a thing or two.

Very late at night, Pronvelle winds down with a light supper of Doritos and rye whiskey. He says a warm Goodnight to his audience and retires to bed. If you check Google Earth in the pre- dawn light, you can see the Mountain Lion thudding his tail in frustration and as he listens to the gentle purrs and snores of Pronvelle and Sneeze tucked up in bed.

ELEVEN

DUDE FALLS IN LOVE AND PENNY DISCOVERS JACOBEAN TRAGEDIES

SECOND LIFE CAN BE a dangerous place for love. Some people fall in and out of love like a dip in the bayou after a drunken night. Some obsess, drive you nuts and then suddenly leave you when some other shiny, bright avatar appears. These are the worst, as they truly believe that they really, really care and then, just as quickly, they forget you exist. We can all tell tales about that. Some men have a whole stable of girlfriends without each being aware of the others. Eventually they all find out and share the information and then he has to disappear till the coast is clear. Women do not forget in a hurry.

Most people are good and true and honest. They are the best sort. But sometimes we misunderstand each other. So when Storm caught Dude with a dewy look in his eye, the alarm bells sounded. Storm knows that in Dude's case, it is usually a very exciting new website that he is drooling over and getting upset is the last thing she should do. It is best to keep occupied until he wanders back and says, 'Hello Dear Heart', in his usual way.

So Storm went off on a trip to visit The Very Superior

Emporium of Millionaire Mij and Princess Nao. Now you have all been in Harrods, I expect, or the Galeries Lafayette in Paris. The Very Superior Emporium looked just like one of these stores. And oh my! They have polished wooden shelves and all the signs are put up straight. Storm's cat shop signs can best be described as higgledy-piggledy. And the cats!! Oh, do they have cats, lotsandlotsandlots of very superior cats. It really is an exquisite shop and Storm bought a very nice Black Russian kitten with genetic traits coming out of his tiny ears.

Now there is Prada and there is Ralph Lauren, one has glass and chrome and the other has leather and hay bales. Storm and Dude's cat shop was in the hay bale category and it suited the Junkyard site. It was warm, and they were proud of it. But there is always a thing or two to be learned from the example of others. So Storm trotted off to the lovely people at KittyCatS, who taught her to label the boxes properly and gave her some tips on traits and breeding. Storm worked into the night, relabeling the boxes and working out the traits of all the cats. She had a glass of her favorite green vodka and saying a quick 'bye bye' to each; she sent the under-performing kitties off to the Menagerie to play with the rare butterflies. Then she planned her strategy and went to tell Dude.

She found him chanting on his island. He listened, and then looked at Storm as if she was a mass-murderer. Bad move, thought Storm. Then he said 'OK, whatever', and got that dewy look in his eye. Storm's heart sank through the sand and her mouth turned down at the corners. Oh dear, oh dear, was it her turn to be abandoned and alone? All went quiet and Storm was just about to go away and be sad by herself when Dude picked up Duvessa, his beautiful devil-cat. Ah yes, he is in love........... again.

In quick succession, one Sunday before she went out to get her nails done, Storm birthed four kittens, Cayden, Braeden, Velvet and Toffee. All were Black Russian with a genetic trait for fold ears or a combination of this. She had once held a Scottish Fold kitten, and it was soft and gentle and she liked it. Fold ears occur when a normal dominant gene mutation makes the ears fold over, and bend forward and down. The heads look nice and round and a bit like an owl.

The new kittens all had lots of genetic traits. They were extremely superior kittens, so they got their own special cushion to sleep on. The rest of the pack thought they looked suspiciously like little black mice, a cross between a takeaway and meals on wheels. They watched the new babies intently. All the new kittens had six or more traits. Braeden was home bred, being the offspring of Dude's cats, Jiselle and Randolph, who was the grandson of Ormond and Bronya, the original cat shop couple now retired to comfy cushions in the fountain courtyard. Cayden had come from the Very Superior Emporium, and Toffee and Velvet were little bargain bin babies. Storm was very pleased with her new kittens and planned to breed the four as a group.

Meanwhile, the Devil-Cats were growing large, hungry and more beautiful each day. Devil- Cats can fly and come equipped with their own personal vehicle that can sweep out the cat shop when not needed for trips. Storm had taken Eckerd for a broomstick ride and ended up falling off the cliff into the ocean. They would not try that again. Eckerd did not like water one little bit and there was a hissing like damp flames. She could just imagine the fuss if Dude's lovely Duvessa had got wet. Duvessa was now the object of all his cuddles. What would the Divine Penny think of that?

The Divine Penny was to be seen reading *The Duchess of Malfi* and other Jacobean blood and lust plays on the spot behind the tent recently vacated by Jiselle and Randolph, now retired to the grassy patch by the pagoda. She may have been learning Italian in case she needed that extra bit of passion. Her head rested defiantly on *The Orgasm Primer*. She was clearly waiting for her moment!

TWELVE

THE KITTENS GO TO UNIVERSITY

AS STORM INTENDED to raise very superior kittens, she thought it would be a good idea to get them an education. Dude was very keen on education and was deeply wrapped up in a MOOC (a Massive Open Online Course) along with twenty-two thousand other people, who were all very excited by the idea of free learning. He went to 'hangouts' to have important discussions. Storm suspected everyone talked at once and they ate international food.

So a curriculum was drawn up. The kittens would study Shakespeare, Art History, and the novels of Jane Austen with Storm, and Dude would take them to the Junkyard University to learn the other stuff, such as Philosophy, Physics and Fishing. Once educated, the kittens would be very valuable and would no doubt develop extra traits and whiskers.

The next question was who should have this splendid educational opportunity? The four Black Russian kittens were the obvious choice. The Devils came with a set of skills that were best not discussed out loud, but seemed to involve frogs and unexplained blood stains. The Divine

Penny was currently studying vendetta, vengeance and knife throwing. The rest of the tribe was generally asleep, so it was best to leave them alone to do their own stuff.

Education was all very well, but universities are full of very odd people with an appalling dress sense who are deeply obsessed with small kernels of knowledge that no one else has noticed. The most important thing is the size and aspect of their office and how many dusty old books can be crammed onto the shelves. Those from the old school sneer terribly at the whiz kids from the digital media, who have an empty white office containing only a computer, a desk and chair, and a coffee machine. They usually keep their bicycle in the doorway and the students climb over it. It pleased Storm that the educators at Junkyard University would properly supervise their kittens.

Next to consider was which language they should learn. Being Black Russian kittens, Storm sort of presumed they were fluent in a Slavic language, but they did not seem to understand when shown the pictures of Marx and Moscow, although they liked the Marx Brothers, but that didn't really count, as the brothers who did actually speak seemed to be American, or Italian or both.

So the kitten's education would be in English. Dude stressed that it was to be English, English and not any other sort and they were not to develop Storm's annoying Emerald City inflections or the East End slang that they both slipped into unawares. Storm agreed the kittens should sound very posh and occasionally drop elegant phrases in French. Dude said she was a daft tart, and they would be very lucky if the cats ever managed to read the label on the Kitty Kibble.

THIRTEEN

HONEY, WE GOT A MEGAPUSS!

THE MEGAPUSS ARE EVERYWHERE and one had knocked Storm over; it being large and bouncy and she being smaller and wobbling on her heels as usual. So the arrival of a huge box had come as a bit of shock. Storm was cuddling Darwin, the beautiful Siamese with the interesting chopped tail and Pamela, the pretty little orange-eyed daughter of the Divine Penny. The two had been partnered and the kitten eagerly expected. Then, as is the way with breedables, there was suddenly a box. Only it was a big box, a very big box. Storm put the two cats gently on the floor and transferred the box to the window ledge where they could view the image and the information about what was inside. There followed a long silence......

Please imagine the 'think' bubbles here:

Dude: *Gawd, I hope she doesn't want to keep this one at my place. It will trample everything. It's a monster!*

Storm: *I don't like these things. They are huge and they push me. I hope Dude won't want me to keep it. It will trample everything.*

Love has a way of making two people think the same

thing at the same time. So when they both said, 'it's a monster' together, they knew there would be no quarrels. It was agreed that the MegaPuss should go into the shop and be priced accordingly. It was a Siamese MegaPuss with lime green eyes and a chopped tail and lots of traits. Someone would buy it soon, they hoped.

Meanwhile, it was time to prepare the shop for Thanksgiving. Now Storm and Dude were not Americans, but they knew this event was deeply treasured by their American friends and so they should reflect that in the shop decorations. So Storm had a rummage in her inventory and found a sizzling turkey and they bought a flag. The idea was to display the kittens enjoying their Thanksgiving Dinner.

When they got to the Junkyard, it was all decked out with big turkeys that looked like crochet cushions. They also had names. Storm and Dude didn't understand this. Dinner was called, well, ...dinner. It seemed unkind to give it a name and then eat it.

'Not the proper form, old thing,' Dude said. Storm said she didn't much care as long as there was something for dinner and she was not an 'old thing', so cut it out. Dude said they should respect the traditions of other countries if they wanted to give their food a name - like McDonald's. Storm said that she only ate unnamed foods. Dude said her food was unnamed because it was inedible and an affectionate little scuffle ensued, ending in cuddles and kisses.

FOURTEEN

THE DEVILS HAVE AN UGLY BABY

'DOODLES!'

'Baby!' squealed Storm with excitement. What she had intended to say was, 'The Devil-Cats have had a kitten.'

'It's a Star!' and Dude meant to say that the baby has arrived in a box shaped like a blue star. They both peered at it.

Storm: *What is it?*

Dude: *Blue Devil.*

Storm (petulantly)**:** *It says on the label that it is Captain Invincible.*

Dude: *What do we do?*

We are getting to the really gritty bit of the exchange, aren't we?

Dude: *This fella looks like he is wearing blue pyjamas or a sweater. Does he have any glowing bits?*

Storm: *Probably, but that might be kind of personal.*

They both stared at it for some time. It was hideous. Dude wriggled uncomfortably and registered a domain:

```
http://thisdamncatisugly.org
```

and then consulted the price lists of other stores hoping

it might be valuable. Even a mother could not love that face. The new box was placed on the window ledge until a decision could be reached as to its fate. Currently, there was no more room in the shop for new cats. Storm thought maybe they could pass it off as Santa in the Christmas display.

During that week, a whole new crop of babies arrived. First, a lovely five trait Siamese with fold ears from Pamela and Darwin and then a pink Château, with rather nice rainbow prism eyes from Hadar and Coconut. The illusive lime-green Siamese were still out of reach. They were placed on the window ledge to await the Christmas display.

Over on the special Black Russian cushion, things were getting a bit out of control. The little black mice now resembled a passing oil slick on the nice white cushion. They were big. Some of them were enormous. Storm did not hug them very much. She was hoping that their allocated partners would do that as she waited for some high-trait babies to arrive. At the moment, her thoughts were focused on Amita, the Buddha of Infinite Light. He was approaching the 120-day mark, and she really wanted another kitten before he took up his permanent job as the resident cat shop pet. Amita was much too gorgeous to be heading to The Menagerie.

Quietly in the background at Dude's place, the Divine Penny is almost 120 days too. No more kittens for her.

'She only has one trait anyway,' Storm remarked, 'And that is her temper.'

The Divine Penny is behind the tent reading Machiavelli and in Italian, too. She is a worry.

FIFTEEN
THE SEARCH FOR THE GOLDEN KITTEN

ONE DAY, Millionaire Mij casually dropped the words 'Golden Kitten' into the conversation. Storm and Dude did not know what this was, but both nodded sagely for the time being. Once back on Dude's island, they consulted the computer in a great hurry. Dude also registered a website in anticipation. Storm thought he was a bit premature, but he said they should be prepared for all eventualities, which was daft, as they didn't know what it was yet. She suggested it could be fifty feet tall with fangs, not a lot of good to them then, was it? The Divine Penny consulted the catalogs of the major international auction houses. She never missed a trick.

Finally, a reference was found:

The Golden Kitten is a lost treasure of the Aztecs. In the 13th century, Mexico was the heart of the Aztec civilization. The Aztecs made a lot of splendid golden objects for their temples and one of these was the now-lost treasure, the legendary Golden Kitten.

Storm peered over Dude's shoulder, admiring the earrings illustrated as 'fabulous Aztec Gold.' If the Golden Kitten was lost, how come Millionaire Mij knew all about it? Storm suspected that Princess Nao may have nipped out to Harrods and got him an artistic copy as an early Christmas present. She suggested to Dude that they might get a replica made for their shop. But Dude was having none of this. He wanted the real thing. He wanted the real Golden Kitten all wrapped in blue and gold paper with bows and ribbons to give to Storm on Christmas morning.

So first he needed a picture of it and a bit of an idea of where to look. He worked on through the night, long after Storm had curled up and gone to sleep, and finally he found what he was looking for, a tiny little drawing of the Golden Kitten.

Cor!

Dude was pretty impressed. Then he read on:

In 1554, a Spanish convoy sets sail from the Veracruz, Mexico, on their homebound voyage to Spain, where merchants awaited the treasures carried on board. Of the four ships, only one was to reach Havana. The remainder met a disastrous fate off the Texas coast. The convoy was halfway through when a terrible storm hit. Three of the ships were swept violently off course and ran aground on the sandbars off Padre Island.

They sent quickly a salvage expedition as the ships were carrying a valuable cargo; sugar, wood, cowhides and dyes, plus gold and silver bullion and precious objects valued at nearly ten million in Spanish currency. One of these objects was the Golden Kitten.

Some of the treasure was recovered, but most was not

accounted for and have, for some four centuries, remained buried undersea, disturbed only by passing hurricanes. Then, in 2005, there was a huge hurricane that sent the treasures floating across the Gulf of Mexico.

Dude eventually fell asleep with his nose on the keyboard. He was dreaming of the Golden Kitten, which may be rather closer than he thought.

SIXTEEN

WE CONSIDER TWEETING AND TWERKING

PROFESSOR MORRIS MODERN held the Progressive Professorial Chair of Media Leeks and Tweeting. Someone suggested he should add Twerking, but he declined, as he did not really understand what it was and he could find no scholarly papers on the subject in the library. It was remarked around the Quad that he would not be much good at it, anyway. M'n'M, as he was known to his students, ventured occasionally into the virtual world of the Cat Shop, but usually retreated quickly because of the shocking state of his avatar. The kittens howled horribly when they saw him coming, consumed with mirth. Storm explained gently that they were happy kittens, hence the laughter. She gave Dude a firm kick as he giggled so that he yelped in pain. M'n'M, was a little concerned that people just kept laughing at him. He thought the green spiky hair, the moon boots and the anti-static blasting gun were pretty cool. His students had a different view and his highly digital, illustrated, virtual world lectures were completely sold out and were voted best academic comedy by the student newspaper.

Tragically marooned in 1990, when he became a Senior Lecturer in Walkman Studies at a remote university, he progressed steadily chair-by-chair, depending on the type of media devices in current use. Once you had one really cool job title, it was relatively easy to get promoted until you reached the dizzy heights of professor and there was nowhere else to go, except totally mad. He had reached the pinnacle of his career and his only regret was that he had not become a rock star. He thought glumly of his receding hairline and abandoned all hope. Careful use of his title usually got him a good table in the restaurant and a nice seat on the plane.

He and Professor Poppett would spend many happy hours discussing the important aspects of their research over a glass of something nice. Generally, it went like this:

Modern: (sadly), *My students laugh at me, Poppett.*

Poppett: *I bet they do, Modern.*

Modern: *I tweet every day and sometimes for twenty minutes at a time.*

Poppett: *I bet you do, Modern.*

There is a silent interlude in which both stare into their glasses. M'n'M imagines hoards of screaming girls ripping their clothes off and lying naked before him. Professor Poppett thinks fondly of her poodle and her eyes glazed over.

Modern: *How is the poodle going on, Poppett?*

Poppett: *Still the same, Modern. As soon as you put it indoors, it goes on and on. No stopping it, not a hope.*

A contemplative pause follows.

Poppett: *Bloody therapist was useless. He ate all my food. Cost a fortune, mind you. Tom, the Media Pet Psycholo-*

gist from Yale, recommended him to me. Behavioral therapist. Not a hope.

Modern: *Oh dear.*

Another silent pause.

Modern: *Do have some more Shiraz, Poppett.*

And so the wheels of intellectual propinquity, both interdisciplinary and multidisciplinary, purred along as they always did. The kittens slept soundly and Dude nursed his sore leg. Storm observed from a safe distance and then sorted the tangles out later when the professorial heads were safely tucked up in their beds.

SEVENTEEN

MEANWHILE, ON THE OTHER SIDE OF THE BAYOU

YOU DON'T REALIZE how big Second Life is until you travel around. You can teleport directly to your destination, but where is the fun in that? It's the journeys that make up our lives and make them meaningful. Storm and Dude had made more journeys than most and really could not remember all the places they had been to, real or virtual.

Millionaire Mij particularly enjoyed his trips to the visit the Maker at the far end of the bayou. He sailed slowly, took one of his cats with him and indulged himself on the journey. Princess Nao made lots of sandwiches and gave him a woolly rug to take in case he got cold or wanted a nap on the way.

The Maker would make anything at a price and if he felt inclined on that particular day. Strenuous activity was not his strong point. His workshop was a place that Millionaire Mij visited when he needed some special display items for his chain of cat shops. Mij was in a good mood. The Christmas decorations were up and he was looking for some items for his next special display. He had been reading a History of Mexico and a small drawing of a cat caught his eye. It was the Golden Kitten. Princess Nao thought a few golden cats would give a bit of an upmarket feel to the stores, so Mij was off to commission the Maker to knock up a few cats with some nice shiny gold paint. He could put some Spanish galleons around with the cats dressed as pirates and a Golden Kitten on a treasure chest with a heap of Spanish gold. He dreamed happily as he enjoyed the peaceful scenery.

The Maker was rather unhygienic, so he got few visitors. He was gray and swamp-like and had a fondness for alligator shoes. His workshop was in a wooden shack by the side of the bayou, far beyond the blue edges of Terrebonne. The Maker's old fishing boat was rotting and rather smelly, not too far from the workshop. The workshop was squashed inside the small shack, and piles of objects spilled out onto the mud flats. When Mij arrived, the Maker was sitting in the sun polishing some newly finished items. Mij approached quietly and squatted close by and waited until the Maker decided it was time to see him. He raised his muddy eyes and grunted a greeting.

'Howdy'.

'How do', said Mij. There was a long pause.

'Y'all right?'

'Alright', said Mij, who was afraid this conversation might go on for hours and not progress.

The Maker fell silent for a while and chewed his cigarillo in silent contemplation. Mij wondered if he was happy, but concluded that he seemed quite relaxed and at ease and really had nothing much to worry about him except the odd bad-tempered alligator. The Maker reached out his hand for the sketch. It was carefully prepared, with measurements and materials written neatly at the bottom. Another silence fell while he studied the drawing. When he thought he had looked enough, he continued with his polishing, deep in thought.

Finally, he said, 'Ten of these gold cats to collect in five days and you pay now if you would.'

Mij handed over his money and politely wished the Maker a good evening. He got no answer. The sun was setting as Mij drifted home. The bayou was beautiful at sunset and his cat dozed next to him in the boat. Princess Nao would be very pleased and he hoped she would give him a nice fish supper.

EIGHTEEN

WE PUT UP THE CHRISTMAS DECORATIONS AND MIJ HAS A LUCKY ESCAPE

IT WAS ALMOST Christmas at **Not Another Kitten** and time for the decorations. Storm had a small tree and lots of boxes and ribbons and some lights and silver stars for the shop doorway. Dude was wearing his best cargo pants stuffed with boxes of tacks and hammers and nails and sticky substances of all types. It was a weekend and lots of new kittens were ready to make an exciting display for the customers. Storm and Dude liked to play and soon Storm was tied to the chair by lengths of ribbon, with lots of bows all over her. This was in retaliation for the silver streamers which she had tied to the back of Dude's belt, leaving him to wander around with a long tail, to everyone's amusement. The pair had now settled down to hug each other better and play nice for a while. Dude thought Storm should have her feet tickled before he let her go free. The Cat Shop shook to the sounds of happy giggles and gently purring sleeping cats.

Meanwhile, Millionaire Mij was on his way to collect his ten replica golden kittens from the Maker. The journey was swift, and he arrived to find a box waiting for him outside the locked workshop. Stuck to the lid was a grubby note. It reads:

Darn alligators - here are your cats - don't hang about.

Mij was unclear if he was to leave quickly because of the alligators or because the Maker was not around to engage him in another stimulating conversation. He decided that the smell from the old fishing boat was rather worse than usual and a wise man would be on his way, so he loaded the box of statues on his boat and started for home. He sailed quickly past the smelly old boat and drifted dreamily along, unaware that he had a bit of an escort floating below the softly lapping waves.

Alligators have terrible breath and shocking tempers. They don't like salt water and prefer aquatic habitats of low salinity, such as lakes and swamps. They also like a nice handy food supply, preferably unsalted, but will eat whatever they fancy. Ask them about pelican or water moccasin, and they will consider both as an equally tasty snack. Humans are not on the menu; just don't get in their way.

The Maker did not like alligators very much. He thought them a pest, and they ate the ducks around his workshop that he regarded as part of his larder. So sometimes the competition between the two top predators turned very nasty. The alligators would bask on the mud flats close to the workshop, discouraging customers and taking the odd snap at the Maker if he came too close. The Maker, in his turn, would rush out of his workshop with his shotgun and fire a few rounds to show them who was the boss. Sometimes he was more accurate than intended and a nice skin for new boots was the result. Before Mij arrived, such an altercation had taken place and the Maker had thought it best to seek some holiday accommodation on dry land for a while and have a trip to see his boot maker. So he left the box for Mij and a note that he hoped would prevent him from staying too long and becoming the subject of a revenge attack. The alligators assumed all humans were the same, which, to an alligator, they were.

It was just as well that Millionaire Mij was descended from an elite sailor and adventurer. He was born and raised in Plymouth, which was a well-known naval port in Elizabethan times. His famous ancestor, Mijack, was a drinking pal of Francis Drake. Together they sailed to South America with letters of marque from Elizabeth I, to plunder the Spanish treasure ships and the intrepid pair became feared by the Spanish fleet as seafarers of dash and dare. On their return to England with tons of treasure, the Queen, delighted by her share of the Spanish plunder, knighted Drake and Mijack. Drake returned to his seafaring ways, but Mijack gave up the sea and bought a friendly pub and lived to enjoy his loot.

Mij was just starting a second chorus of his favorite nautical song when the boat got a little bump. He looked over the side and, seeing nothing, assumed it was a log floating in the bayou. He settled down and a few seconds later, there was another bump on the other side of the boat. Sharper bumps from the front quickly followed this. Suddenly Mij knew he was under attack. His stern profile resembled his illustrious ancestor as he focused all his attention on steering the boat. Looking to one side, he could see the shapes of the alligators swimming just below the surface as they renewed their assault on the little boat. They were intent on turning his small boat over and wreaking their revenge on him. He thought about Princess Nao and how she would be embarrassed if an alligator ate him. She would probably be very upset, too.

What he needed was a weapon. Some hand grenades,

perhaps. He looked around the boat and his eye fell on the box of kitten statues. They were metal and weighty and a good throwing shape too. He wrenched off the lid and aimed a kitten squarely at the head of the closest reptile. Alligators don't yelp, but it was such an excellent shot that it certainly flinched and backed off a bit. Taking another kitten in his hand, he aimed it at the alligator behind him. After another three or four missiles, the alligators were getting the message, and by the time the box was empty, Mij was in clear water and sailing briskly for home with a good tale to tell at dinner.

On serious reflection, he thought he would forget golden kittens and just have some pirate treasure and sailing ships in the next display. He might have a model of his famous ancestor storming the Spanish fleet. The bayou was littered with ten replica kittens and the swell of the waves and the swish of the alligators were pushing them closer to the shoreline.

NINETEEN

PROFESSOR POPPETT'S POODLE
GETS A POSH COAT

PROFESSOR POPPETT WAS INVITED to spend Christmas at Professor Modern's very superior residence in the mountains. This would involve a splendid feast. And the very best thing of all was pets were invited too. M'n'M knew if he didn't invite the pets, everyone would find an excuse to stay at home and watch Game of Thrones secretly. Invite the pets and they would all come and watch the reruns of his TED Talk and his appearance on University Challenge in 1973. The Professor was a wonderful host who wined and dined his guests in the manner of a bygone age. Everyone had to dress for dinner and they played croquet on the lawn. He booked the caterers and name-dropped the chef's name in fluent Japanese. He also dropped casually the name of the celebrity vet with the bouncy blonde wig who would be present and didn't mind being pestered for advice on fleas. Now he was pretty well sure of a full house and lots of Christmas presents.

The mountains were rather chilly at this season and Professor Poppett, being occupied with rowing, running, writing, and directing the universe, completely forgot and sent beloved poodle for his regular clip and toenails. Something had to be done. Beloved poodle would be cold in the mountains and the RSVP had already been sent.

So the next morning, Storm arrived as usual to find a large poodle sitting at her desk neatly curled in the chair. An email was sent from the adjoining office requesting a priority search for cashmere poodle coats in Royal Stewart tartan. It appeared that the poodle was required to have a matching outfit as the Professor had decided to wear something a bit Vivienne Westwood for the formal dinner. Storm rather enjoyed performing extremely difficult tasks. First she calculated the days until the event and the delivery time by courier from various exclusive stores world-wide who might stock such an item. This would be a tight deadline and before hitting the phone, she ordered a supply of dinners for the cats and left Dude instructions to fend for himself.

Several hours and much giggling later, Storm had managed the impossible.

A beautiful tartan coat that your pet will be proud of; it features a toggle fastening with a contrasting black tartan yoke at the back. It is fleece-lined with a hood to keep your pup snug. Your pet will be a serious style icon.

Storm wiped the tears of laughter from her eyes and completed the purchase by adding a knitted Argyle sweater with a red and white diamond pattern. Sweetie of the Pet Couture department at the House of Dogue reliably informed her, that the Argyle pattern had seen a resurgence in popularity in the last few years because of its adoption by a luxury clothing manufacturer in Scotland.

She booked the international courier to collect the

parcels and, having made sure beloved poodle had inspected the photographs and sniffed them in approval, she expertly flicked the adored pet on the floor and sat down and got covered in pet hairs.

Then she leaned on her desk and wondered what Dude was up to, how the cats were doing and a thousand other things that really did not matter a jot in the scheme of things. He had been secretive of late. She hoped he was not doing anything daft, or going too close to the edge of the bayou and teasing the alligators.

TWENTY

THE GOLDEN KITTEN IS FOUND AND SNATCHED

WHILE STORM WAS DEALING with the fashion requirements of Professor Poppett's poodle, Dude thought he might go fishing. He took his boat and some bait and Penny came along for company, as she often did when Storm was not around. Joyous Joy stopped by in her sailboat, CupCake, to say good day and told him alligators had chased that Mij and he had to throw things to fend them off. Dude's ears perked up as he asked Joy to tell him the story. Joy was vague, having got the story at sixth or seventh hand. She just knew that Mij had thrown heavy metal objects at them and was such an excellent shot that he was now captain of the bowls team.

Joy's boat skipped away to enjoy the sun on the bayou and Dude got to thinking. His thoughts went like this; heavy metal objects out in the bayou might be the Spanish treasure. Old saucepans and bicycle frames did not figure high in his thinking. Dude was thinking what his imagination wanted him to think, and for the purposes of this story, he was right.

He hauled in his fishing tackle, placed Penny gently at

the prow of the boat, where she could play at being on the Titanic and set sail for Terrebonne, the rough location of the alligator attack. He sailed close to the shoreline, looping around the islands and watching carefully for alligators in case they were still a bit miffed with mankind.

Then, as he rounded an island corner, he saw something gleaming in the mud, almost hidden by the swamp grass. Dude had a healthy respect for reptiles so keeping a sharp lookout, he moored the boat and stepped over the side and immediately fell headfirst into the mud. He distinctly heard Penny laugh, and he grinned back at her as her intense blue eyes watched his every move. Picking himself up, he grabbed on to the grasses at the bayou's edge and a heavy object literally fell into his hand. It was round and golden and beautifully warm.

It was the **Golden Kitten**!

Dude gave a whoop of delight and leapt back in the boat and did a bit of a dance. He rinsed the statue in some water, then wrapping it in a towel, he turned the boat and started for home, where he planned to wash and polish himself and the statue. As he hummed his way along, he might have noticed if he had looked, that hidden in the shoreline grasses were several other bright objects. Littered around the bayou, just waiting to be found, were another *ten* golden statues.

Knowing that Storm was away, Dude went first to the Cat Shop, as he could moor his boat close by. Once inside, with his feet on the display table and Penny watching him from on top of the Christmas display, he polished the statue.

He would use one of the spare display boxes to wrap and ribbon Storm's Christmas gift. She probably peeped at the presents under the tree, so he would hide the gift in the shop until Christmas morning. He imagined her delighted face and the kiss he would get from her, when a huge dark shadow appeared in the doorway. Penny shot under the Christmas tree and the rest of the kittens wailed faintly from inside their boxes.

It was Texan Bugg!

Dude knew he was not there to buy a kitten and anyway, he would not send a kitten home with Texan Bugg. Its little cries would break his heart. Texan Bugg was just lurking around. He liked to know what was happening, and he had no doubt heard about Mij and the alligators. Texan Bugg never missed a trick. So as he came up behind Dude, who quickly dropped the Golden Kitten into the open gift box and replaced the lid, it struck him as being a bit suspicious.

They exchanged pleasantries, well actually more like un-pleasantries in the form of a series of grunts. Dude assumed the stance of the shop owner, despite being covered in mud, by tucking his hands in an imaginary waistcoat. Texan Bugg was not fooled and straightened up to his full height and towered menacingly over Dude. The shop vibrated with trembling kittens and the sounds of their whimpers. The two faced off in silence.

Just at that moment, a throng of customers arrived and while Dude was meeting and greeting, Texan Bugg slyly dipped his hand into the box and felt around. His hand caught something metal and smooth and while Dude's head was turned, he quietly removed the Golden Kitten and made for the door. His thinking was that objects found in the bayou belonged to everyone and he would just inspect whatever it was. He had not noticed that Penny was hiding under the Christmas tree, and she now bravely crawled out and tried to trip him up. Texan Bugg gasped, but regained his footing and quickly headed off.

At that moment, Dude turned his head and realized that the statue was gone. Leaving his customers, he raced for the door, only to see Texan Bugg striding and swaggering along the canal pathway. Feeling like he was the hero in a movie, he started his imaginary car chase, (minus the car), closely followed by Penny, who soon was racing along beside him. Dude had found the Golden Kitten, and he was not giving it up to Texan Bugg.

Observers would have seen a large man with a bright gold kitten, a smaller man covered in mud, and a chocolate Siamese all heading off towards the edge of the bayou, watched by astounded onlookers and startled pelicans.

TWENTY-ONE

PENNY'S LAST LEAP

A LINE of curious pelicans watched as the weird procession raced towards the denser part of the swamp. Texan Bugg was speedy, but the bayou was not a good place to run, there being roots and twists of the Ancient Virginia Oaks hampering his progress. Penny was fast catching up with him and doing all she could to annoy and confuse him. So, while watching her, he tripped and smacked into a tree. He stopped to catch his breath as Dude got closer and closer.

Texan Bugg was not really a violent man, but he was big and tended to wave his arms around, like he was swatting an imaginary fly. As he turned to run from Dude, he swung his arms to give himself traction in the mud and the Golden Kitten flew out of his hand and hit Dude square between the eyes. Dude dropped like a stone and the golden statue landed in his lap. Deciding it was time to disappear, Texan Bugg glanced over his shoulder and realizing from his faint movements that Dude was simply stunned, he had made his getaway. Penny had very different ideas. She was only a cat, a super intelligent, Italian-speaking, well-educated cat, and the love of her little life was lying in an inert heap, groaning painfully. She growled menacingly with all the ferocious intent of an angry tiger.

Then she launched herself with all her strength from her four delicate chocolate paws and landed claws extended on Texan Bugg's vast back. He screamed out in pain and fought to get her off, flailing his arms around himself. Penny clung on with all her might, knowing only that she must hold on until Dude woke up and could defend himself. She could see him from one corner of her eye as he slowly sat up and looked at her, the Golden Kitten still in his lap.

Texan Bugg continued to scream and finally, with all his might, he swung his enormous arm around and caught Penny by the neck. And then suddenly it was all over. He squeezed with all his might and the delicate Siamese was dashed to the ground in a heap of creamy fur. Then, free of his tormentor, Texan Bugg, still howling in pain and rage, took off into the swamp.

Everything was still. The Divine Penny was no more. Dude crawled over and cradled her in his arms and wept for a long time.

Later he dug a little grave in a quiet spot under a big Virginia Oak and placed large stones on top to keep her safe. But Penny deserved more and looking around for something special to mark the spot, his eye fell on the Golden Kitten and he knew it belonged to Penny. He placed it carefully, cementing it firmly with mud from the swamp. Then, saying a quiet goodbye, he turned for home and Storm's comforting kisses.

TWENTY-TWO
HOME FOR CHRISTMAS

DUDE MADE his way slowly and sadly home. He had no present for Storm, and his lovely Penny was gone. He sat alone for a very long time. He didn't want to tell Storm just yet.

Storm was wondering where Penny had got to. She had an idea that Penny would be heading off to make her fortune soon and she liked to imagine her sitting on the steps of Prada on the Via dei Condotti in Rome with her fur gleaming and brushed. Penny would be waiting for the owner of the store to arrive and seeing the delicate chocolate paws and bright blue eyes, he would invite her in for a saucer of cream and a nice career in fashion, sleeping in the window as part of the handbag display. Dude would miss her very much.

Dude went alone to his island and washed the mud from his face and put some plasters on his bumps and scrapes. He was all in one piece, thanks to Penny, and Storm would understand if he didn't explain just yet. She would know. He washed his muddy clothes and rinsing the thick swamp mud out of his pockets, he found two small scraps of metal.

He was about to throw them away, but something made him take a closer look. He rinsed the mud away and found he had two small, delicate gold earrings, a bit like the ones Storm had admired on the website. Perhaps they were the lost Aztec treasure. He didn't think so, but he knew Storm would like them and put them in a small box tied with a bow. He had no Golden Kitten to give her, but he thought she would be content.

Next day, Storm went across to the Cat Shop and in the pride of place in the Christmas display was a beautiful choco-late point Siamese kitten with lovely big green eyes and a nice, wriggly tail. It had nine traits, so it was very fine. She put a bow around its neck and a label that said, *To Dude, with love and kisses from Storm.* The new little girl would not replace the Divine Penny, but she would make him smile again.

On Christmas Eve, the two put their presents under the big Christmas tree at Storm's house. They dressed in their best, tucked the kittens up for the night and, holding hands, they went to dance together under the full moon. On Christmas morning, they opened their presents, and the kittens raced around tearing up silver and gold paper and getting their paws tangled in the ribbons. Storm looked pretty in her new earrings and Dude registered a domain to celebrate. Dude's new kitten was pert and perky and was called Morgana. She was one of Penny's daughters. They were delighted with their presents. They smiled because they had each other to love, which was the best gift of all.

By, now the ten Golden Kittens had become mythology and were eventually all collected and donated to the Junk-yard University to be used as paperweights when the breeze blew too briskly around the bayou. Everyone thought it fit that the golden statue should watch over the brave Penny and left flowers when they passed that way. No one did the sums and if they did, they assumed the Maker, having failed his course in basic accounting, had made an extra statue.

But we know, don't we?

TWENTY-THREE
TEXAN BUGG MEETS HIS HORRIBLE FATE

AFTER HIS FRANTIC retreat to the swampy end of the bayou, Texan Bugg was not seen for a long time. Life went on. His name came off the DJ schedule, but no one took much notice. He frequently went off suddenly and returned months later. Recently at the full moon, there had been heard the distant sound of wailing out in the bayou.

Storm was really a kind person so one night when Dude was asleep; she packed a picnic basket with jalapeño sandwiches and set off into the misty night. Eckerd, her devoted Devil-Cat, was fully grown and his tail also glowed in the dark, a useful attribute at night. He had sharp fangs so if Texan Bugg gave her any trouble, he could be sure of a nasty bite.

The bayou was very beautiful at night and the alligators lived on a plentiful diet of plump pelicans, so you were pretty safe unless you were a pelican. Anyway, Devil-Cats can fly, so Storm would come to no harm. She was adored and protected. She moved slowly by the glow of Eckerd's tail as the moon had not yet risen.

Suddenly, she heard an awful gurgling and moaning not too far ahead. Eckerd's claws padded gently on her shoulder in a warning and Storm dropped onto all fours after first selecting a soft, clean patch of swamp grass. The sound was coming from directly ahead, a sort of swampy, gurgling noise, like a hippopotamus in a mud bath. Just then, an owl screeched and the full moon rose over the water. Storm was mainly occupied with wondering how to get the sandwiches to Texan Bugg without going closer and getting stuck in the mud.

Only when the moaning started again she looked up and silhouetted against the moon was the monstrous shape of Texan Bugg. His lower half was stuck in the fast drying quicksand up to his waist. His braces were caught on an overhanging branch of a cypress tree. He could go neither up nor down. He was stuck for eternity in a hot tub of swamp mud. He would die of starvation unless the alligators ran out of plump pelicans and were so desperate as to eat him instead.

Suddenly, he moved sharply to one side and snatched at something in the dark. In the moonlight, Storm saw his big sausage fingers clasping something round and wriggling. It was a huge swamp cockroach. She turned her head quickly so as not to see his gaping jaws close around the helpless insect. Texan Bugg was not going to starve anytime soon.

As she crawled quickly away, the air filled with a horrible gurgling chuckle; Texan Bugg had eaten his dinner. When she was out of sight, she stood up and walked back slowly in the warm moonlight. Close to her ear were the joyful sounds of Eckerd crunching on the jalapeño sandwiches.

The End.......but is it? They say that a cat has nine lives.

Enter the world of the **CyberCat Series**, and meet Penny, a one-of-a-kind Siamese Cat with an independent streak, nine mythical lives, and the right amount of attitude to keep things interesting. Follow her as she navigates diverse worlds and ages, extending a helpful chocolate-coloured paw and leaving an indelible mark on the hearts of those she meets.

Fun and fright in the Gothic splendour of a university in Sydney. **The University Cat: A Tale for Grown-Ups and Graduates** comes alive when an exuberant poodle puppy leaps over the writer's desk, igniting a thrilling escapade celebrating the quirks of some remarkable academics and their friends in Australia.

The CyberCat finds herself in Shakespeare's London and meets the man himself. **Beware the Cat: The Shakespearean Chronicles** draws inspiration from a fascinating piece of early English literature, combining historical intrigue with contemporary wit. Populated with historic characters and a mischievous feline who has slipped through time, it weaves a tale of an exhilarating yet perilous age.

The Reluctant Gift launches Penny, the CyberCat, into another enthralling adventure, this time captivating the crowds as she becomes an exhibit in Victorian London's most spectacular showcase; the Great Exhibition of 1851. As Penny navigates this perplexing world, she becomes entangled in a high-stakes adventure to prevent the theft of a priceless brooch.

In **The Greening of Ginger George**, Penny returns to her comfortable home in Australia, but a violent storm and a strange new kitten disrupt her life. Penny joins the fight against unscrupulous developers who want to turn the forest into a spa for rich tourists.

Explore the series' origins with **Tails from the Cat Shop: The Kitten's Story**, a prequel set in a virtual world that blurs the lines between reality and imagination.

Jessika Jenvieve is the pen name of crime writer, Jan Sayer.

For more in the CyberCat Series, sign up for my mailing list: https://www.jansayer.com/